The Twelve Days of Christmas

Illustrated by Susan J. Harrison

![Ideals logo] Ideals Children's Books • Nashville, Tennessee

Copyright © 1989 by Hambleton-Hill Publishing, Inc.
All rights reserved.
Published by Ideals Children's Books
An imprint of Hambleton-Hill Publishing, Inc.
Nashville, Tennessee 37218
Printed and bound in the United States of America

ISBN 1-57102-078-0

On the first day of Christmas my true love gave to me

a partridge in a pear tree.

On the second day of Christmas my true love gave to me

two turtledoves
and a partridge in a pear tree.

On the third day of Christmas my true love gave to me

three french hens,

two turtledoves,
and
a partridge in a pear tree.

On the fourth day of Christmas my true love gave to me

four calling birds,

three french hens,
two turtledoves,
and
a partridge in a pear tree.

On the fifth day of Christmas my true love gave to me

five golden rings,

four calling birds,
three french hens,
two turtledoves,
and
a partridge in a pear tree.

On the sixth day of Christmas my true love gave to me

six geese a-laying,

five golden rings,
four calling birds,
three french hens,
two turtledoves,
and
a partridge in a pear tree.

On the seventh day of Christmas my true love gave to me

seven swans a-swimming,

six geese a-laying,
five golden rings,
four calling birds,
three french hens,
two turtledoves,
and
a partridge in a pear tree.

On the eighth day of Christmas my true love gave to me

eight maids a-milking,

seven swans a-swimming,
six geese a-laying,
five golden rings,
four calling birds,
three french hens,
two turtledoves,
and
a partridge in a pear tree.

On the ninth day of Christmas my true love gave to me

nine drummers drumming,

eight maids a-milking,
seven swans a-swimming,
six geese a-laying,
five golden rings,
four calling birds,
three french hens,
two turtledoves,
and
a partridge in a pear tree.

On the tenth day of Christmas my true love gave to me

ten pipers piping,

nine drummers drumming,
eight maids a-milking,
seven swans a-swimming,
six geese a-laying,
five golden rings,
four calling birds,
three french hens,
two turtledoves,
and
a partridge in a pear tree.

On the eleventh day of Christmas my true love gave to me

eleven ladies dancing,

nine drummers drumming,
eight maids a-milking,
seven swans a-swimming,
six geese a-laying,
five golden rings,
four calling birds,
three french hens,
two turtledoves,
and
a partridge in a pear tree.

On the eleventh day of Christmas my true love gave to me

eleven ladies dancing,

ten pipers piping,
nine drummers drumming,
eight maids a-milking,
seven swans a-swimming,
six geese a-laying,
five golden rings,
four calling birds,
three french hens,
two turtledoves,
and
a partridge in a pear tree.

twelve lords a-leaping,

On the twelfth day of Christmas my true love gave to me

eleven ladies dancing,
ten pipers piping,
nine drummers drumming,
eight maids a-milking,
seven swans a-swimming,
six geese a-laying,
five golden rings,
four calling birds,
three french hens,
two turtledoves,
and
a partridge in a pear tree.

The Twelve Days of Christmas

ENGLAND

Festively

1. On the first day of Christ- mas my true love sent to me A par- tridge_ in a pear tree.

2. On the sec- ond day of Christ- mas my true love sent to me
3. On the third ___ (etc.)
4. On the fourth ___ (etc.)

2, 3, 4. two tur- tle- doves and a par- tridge_ in a pear tree.
3, 4. three french ___ hens,
4. four call- ing birds,

(Sing in reverse order for verses indicated)

5. On the fifth day of Christ- mas my true love sent to me
6. On the sixth
(etc. through twelfth)

6, 7, 8, 9, 10, 11, 12. six geese a- lay- ing, five gold- en rings,
7, 8, 9, 10, 11, 12. seven swans a- swim- ming,
8, 9, 10, 11, 12. eight maids a- milk- ing,
9, 10, 11, 12. nine drum- mers drum- ming,
10, 11, 12. ten pip- ers pip- ing,
11, 12. eleven la- dies danc- ing,
12. twelve lords a- leap- ing,

(Sing in reverse order for verses indicated)

four_ call- ing birds, three french hens, two_ tur- tle- doves, and a par- tridge_ in a pear tree.